BRAIN GAMES™ kids

PICTURE PUZZLES

D1396744

Publications International, Ltd.

Image Sources: Artville, Bananastock, Corbis RF, Dreamstime, Image Source, iStock, Jupiter Images Unlimited, Photodisc, Shutterstock, Stockbyte, Superstock

Contributing Writers: Holli Fort, Laura Pearson

Front cover puzzle: *Soccer Shuffle,* see pages 98–99.
Back cover puzzle: *Knickknack Attack,* see page 136.

Louis Weber, CEO
Publications International, Ltd.
7373 North Cicero Avenue
Lincolnwood, Illinois 60712

ISBN-13: 978-1-4508-1711-0
ISBN-10: 1-4508-1711-4

Manufactured in China.

8 7 6 5 4 3 2 1

A Picture's Worth a Pile of Fun! ■ 4

Start this picture-loving adventure off right with these nice and easy puzzles.

Look a little closer at these action-packed scenes—the search is starting to get harder.

We're really boosting the challenge in this level—make sure you have your game face on!

Buckle up and get ready for the hunt—the last level has the most difficult differences.

A Picture's Worth a Pile of Fun!

To solve a picture puzzle, all you have to do is find the differences between a couple of colorful photos. Piece of cake, right? Well, actually, it can be pretty tricky. First, notice how many changes there are between the photos in each puzzle. You'll find that number in the corner of the page. Then, your best bet is to compare the pictures carefully. You might start by seeing if anything jumps out at you: Maybe there's a new cloud in the sky, or the kid wearing roller skates is suddenly on a skateboard. After that, you'll need to take a very close look at every inch of the picture to find the more subtle, sneaky changes, like socks that changed to a different shade of blue, or a seashell that mysteriously moved across the beach. If you're stumped, don't forget that you can find the solutions by flipping to the answers section in the back of the book.

For some of the puzzles, we've mixed things up by using either four or six pictures that look almost the same. The trick to solving these is to find the one photo out of the bunch that has a single difference from the others. Again, you'll have to look carefully to spot the change!

An important thing to keep in mind is that these puzzles get harder—but even more fun!—as you work through each level. Younger kids might feel that levels 1 and 2 are a perfect fit, but they might not be ready for the higher levels just yet. But that's okay—the more you practice, the better you'll get! And soon you'll be ready to take on the really subtle differences in levels 3 and 4. There's only one way to find out: Take a deep breath, and dive right in to *Brain Games*™ *Kids: Picture Puzzles*!

Masterpiece Matching

We have drawn the conclusion that there are changes between these pictures.
Can you find them all?

4 changes

Toys on Parade

Spring into action as you search for all of the differences!

Answers on page 169.

A New Sheriff in Town

Someone was horsing around and changed this scene.
Can you be the top cop and find all of the differences?

A Few of My Favorite Things

Don't just toy with this puzzle—
keep playing until you've found all of the changes!

Queen of the Bubble Makers

You'll rule the tribe if you find all of the changes between these pictures!

Answers on page 169.

Bumblebee Mystery

Some busy bees have been making changes to this picture.
You'll be flying high when you've found them all!

Piñata Party

Go ahead, take a swipe at finding all of the differences between these scenes.

Answers on page 170.

Greenhouse Guesser

Changes are a-bloom! Can you find them all?

Answers on page 170.

Seashore Stumper

Don't let the sun blind you! Find the single change in one of the pictures below.

1

2

3

4

Answer on page 170 .

Monkeying Around

Try to hang in there until you've found all of the changes in this puzzle.

To the Sky and Back

Don't let your fear of heights stop you from
finding the differences in these pictures!

Answers on page 170

Answers on page 170.

Art Astray

Can you draw up a list of the changes between these pictures?

Answers on page 170.

Push/Pull Puzzle

Take a spin through these scenes, and see how many changes you can round up. **4 changes**

Answers on page 171.

Playroom Puzzle

Can you spell out a list of the differences in these playrooms?

Answers on page 171.

Costume Caper

Play around with this puzzle until you've spotted all of the differences.

Tire Swing Teaser

Finding all of the changes between these scenes shouldn't tire you out!

Answers on page 171.

Unburied Treasure

1 change Can you dig up the single change we've buried among these photos?

1

2

3

4

Answer on page 171.

Summer Vacation Time!

We're *shore* you'll have no trouble landing a list of all the changes.

4 changes

Under My Umbrella

We've sprinkled this picture with changes. Can you find them all?

Answers on page 172.

Family Portrait

There have been changes penciled in to this drawing. Can you find them all?

Answers on page 172.

River Walk

Changes are just streaming through this scene. Can you catch them all?

Gummi Game

It'll be sweet as candy when you find the
one change we've hidden among these photos.

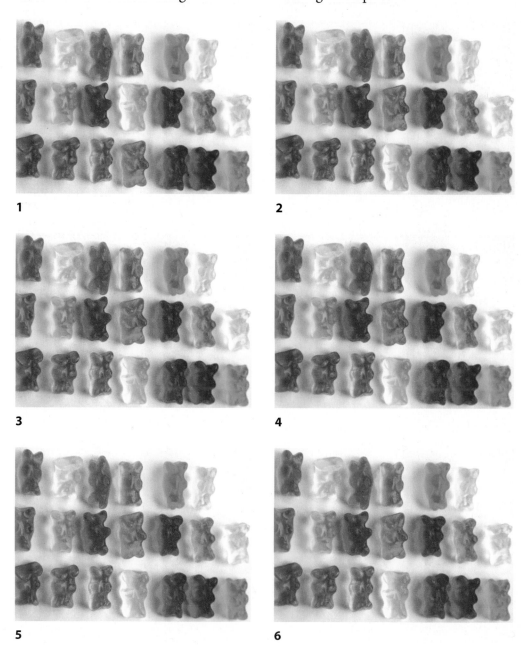

1

2

3

4

5

6

Answer on page 172.

Go Fly a Kite

You'll be flying high once you find all of these changes.

Answers on page 172.

Shoe Swap

Don't go dotty trying to spot all of the changes here!

Answers on page 172.

Tent Twist

Some adjustments have been made to this outdoor adventure.
Camp out with this puzzle until you've found them all.

Dance Demonstration

Do you have the right moves to find the single
change we've hidden among these photos?

1

2

3

4

5

6

Answer on page 173.

A Sandy Search

We've made some monster-size changes to this scene. Can you dig them all up?   **4 changes**

Answers on page 173.

Guitar Guesser

We've added a string of changes to this scene.

Don't fret, we're sure you can find them all!

Answers on page 173.

Chalk Caper

You can chalk it up to experience, but we're guessing that
you won't have any trouble finding all the differences here.

Answers on page 173.

Freeze!

Feeling like you're under fire?
Solving this puzzle should bring you into the clear!

Still Life with Flowers

Changes have sprouted up all over this scene! Can you sniff them out?

Answers on page 174.

A Study in Blues

Can you go long and catch all of the differences in these scenes?

Sock It to Me!

4 changes You'll feel warm and cozy right down to your toes once you finish this puzzle.

Answers on page 174.

Fishbowl Finder

Not to bait you or anything, but we think you'll get hooked
trying to find the one change among these photos.

1

2

3

4

5

6

Answer on page 174.

The Family that Nests Together...

4 changes We've nestled a few changes into this family portrait. Can you find them all?

Answers on page 174.

Heart-ily Yours

We'd love it with all our hearts if you could find all of the differences.

Answers on page 174.

Children's Place

This children's room has undergone a mini-makeover!
See if you can spot the renovations.

Homework Helpers

Homework shared is homework divided—study this picture to find all of the changes.

Answers on page 175.

Stamping Stampede

Don't be stumped by the colorful changes in this stamping scene.

LEVEL 2

Pillow Puzzler

5 changes There's nothing like the friendship between a girl, her dog, and . . . a bunch of animal-print pillows! Can you sniff out all of the changes between these pictures?

Answers on page 175.

Dino Duel

Time to get prehistoric! Can you find the single
evolution we've made among these photos?

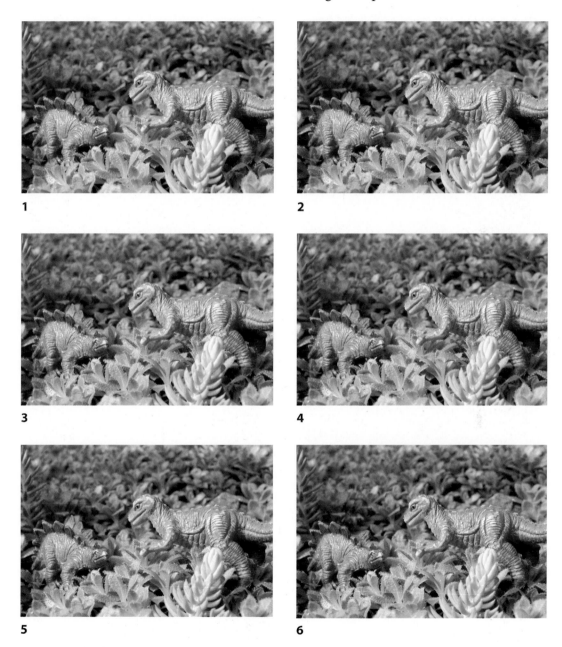

1

2

3

4

5

6

Answer on page 175.

Kids' Carnival

These children are about to take the ride of their lives!
Strap in and get ready for the thrill of solving this puzzle.

Answers on page 175.

Hitters' Huddle

Gather 'round as many changes as you can find between these softball scenes. **5 changes**

Answers on page 176.

Skate Park

5 changes The lone skateboarder in this park is having the time of his life, but change is wheeling along. Can you roll with the punches to find all of the differences?

Answers on page 176.

Pasture Puzzler

Find the single change hidden among these photos
before you get put out to pasture!

1 change

1

2

3

4

5

6

Toy Task

Sort through these dolls and toys, and you'll have no problem
finding all of the changes between these scenes.

Answers on page 176.

In a Class of Their Own

During indoor recess, the classroom becomes a playground.
Can you find all the ways we've played around with this photo?

Answers on page 176.

Meadow Mix-Up

Hopping around the lily pads might help you locate the changes.
Can you find them all?

Karaoke Kraze

5 changes   Finding all the changes in this puzzle will make your brain sing with glee!

Family Fun Find

Can you sketch out a list of the changes between these photos?

Answers on page 177.

Handy Candy Hunt

You'll have your hands full trying to spot the single change
we've made among these pictures!

1

2

3

4

Beauty Mask Task

5 changes   Play beauty parlor with these masked gals, and find all the polished changes.

Answers on page 177.

Up, Up, and Away!

Some changes have been made to the balloon lineup in each picture.
Enjoy the ride as you solve this puzzle!

5 changes

Pencil Me In!

5 changes You'll be feeling pretty crafty once you've drawn up a list of these changes.

Answers on page 177.

Coin Count

Count your pennies! It's time to go all in to find the changes.

LEVEL 2

5 changes

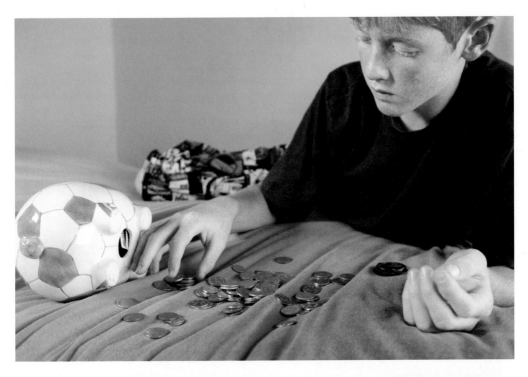

Bunny Brainteaser

Hop to it! Find the one change we've hidden among these silly card-playing rabbits.

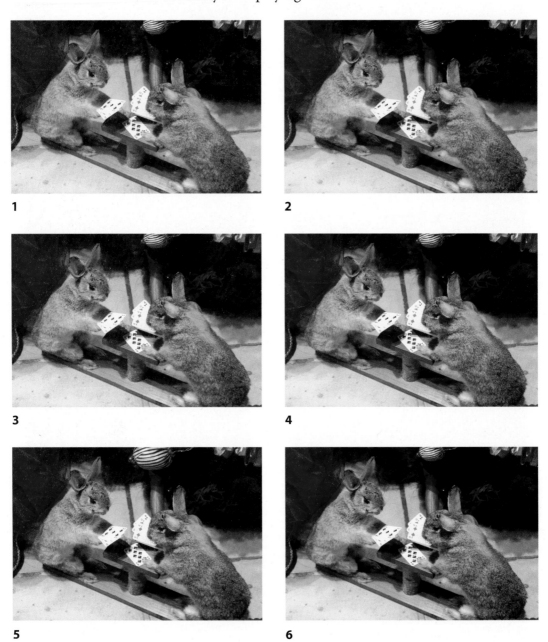

1

2

3

4

5

6

Answer on page 178.

Level 2 banner appears.

Girls' Night In

Can you gather up the changes in these sweet scenes before the ice cream melts? **5 changes**

LEVEL 2

Painting Party

Grab your paint set, and play along by finding all the artistic differences.

Answers on page 178.

Multiply and Divide

Don't split until you've found the changes between these tricky math scenes.

5 changes

Traveling Team

Come along with this brother-and-sister team.
Solving this puzzle may turn out to be a real journey!

Doggie's New Tricks

Be sure to *paws* and search carefully to track down all of the changes.

A Sweeping Performance

Make it a clean sweep with this fun-loving family by spotting all of the differences.

Studio Search

5 changes   You'll find inspiration in every corner as you scour this studio for changes.

Answers on page 179.

Coney Island Cones

Cone you find the one sweet change we've hidden among these pictures?

1

2

3

4

5

6

1 change

When It Rains, It Pours

Can you find the shower of changes we've sprinkled through these scenes?

Geographical Goof

Can you map out the changes between these classroom scenes?

Answers on page 179.

Guinea Pig Guesser

Just look closely to find all the changes in these furry creatures' habitat.

5 changes

Stuffed Shelves

These shelves are crammed with changes! Can you find them all?

Answers on page 180.

Splash-tacular!

Ride a wave of accomplishment as you find all of these changes.

A Quick Study

Examine these pictures carefully.
You'll earn top marks if you find all the changes!

Answers on page 180.

Guitar Heroines

Air out the list of changes to these singing scenes.

Turtle Teaser

You may want to hide in your shell until you spot the single change hidden among these photos, but we're sure you can do it!

1

2

3

4

5

6

Answer on page 180.

Block Party

We've toyed with this photo, and now it's different.
Wanna play along and find all the changes?

6 changes

Answers on page 181.

Kitchen Renovations

We've rearranged a few things in the kitchen and made some changes.
Can you cook up a solution to this puzzle?

Answers on page 181.

Skate-o-Rama

It's fun on wheels at this skate park and festival! Ride the mental rails as you search for the differences between these photos.

Costume Party

You can have your cake and eat it, too—just spot the differences
between these playful party scenes.

Dolly Doozy

This is a dollmaker's dream!
Before playtime, see if you can find all the changes.

Answers on page 181.

Splatter Pattern

Make a splash by finding the one change hidden in these works of art.

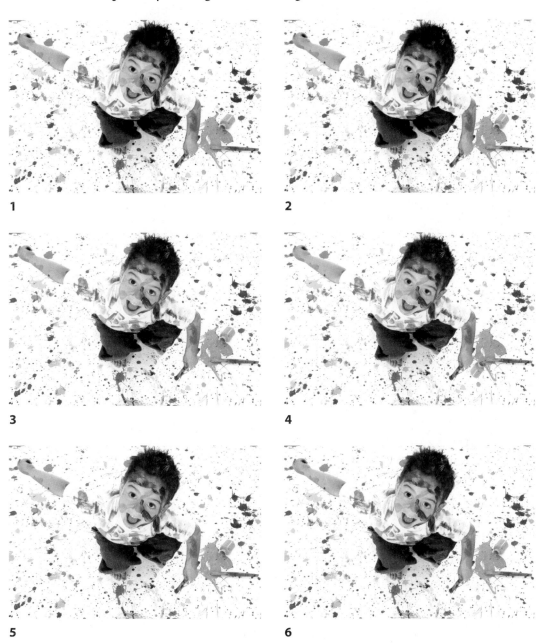

1

2

3

4

5

6

Sledding Switcheroo

Make tracks in a race to the finish as you search for all
of the changes between these two sledding scenes.

Answers on page 182.

Boot Shoot

We've made several changes to this *boot*-iful photo. Can you find them all? **6 changes**

Hula Hunt

6 changes Swivel your eyes all around this puzzle until you've spotted all of the changes.

Answers on page 182.

Study Hall

No need for a tutor—we're sure you'll ace this puzzle just fine on your own.   **6 changes**

Soccer Shuffle

The goal here is to score as many changes as possible.

Googly-Eyed Game

Don't go bug-eyed trying to locate all of the changes in these scenes!

Answers on page 182.

Canoe Caper

Stay on course to bring all of these changes to the surface.

Answers on page 183.

Fountain Fluke

It'll be a real treat to find all of these changes!

Answers on page 183.

Robot Parade

Don't malfunction—find the single change hidden among these mechanical scenes.   **1 change**

1

2

3

4

5

6

Answer on page 183.

Guitar Greats

Tune up your puzzling skills—you'll need them for this one!

104

Candy, Candy in a Dish...

...How many changes do you wish?

Answers on page 183.

A Puzzling Event

Can you piece together the changes between these scenes?

6 changes

Lane Change

6 changes   Can you spare the time to get a strike by finding all of the differences?

Answers on page 184.

School Bus Search

Come aboard to seek out the differences!

Take It Easy

6 changes

What could be better than eating candy and couch surfing?
We hope you can channel enough energy to find all the changes.

Answers on page 184.

Plush Toy Puzzle

These soft plush toys are great to cuddle up with on a cold day!
Curl up in your most comfortable chair, and find all the changes, too.

6 changes

Landscaper's Challenge
Can you weed out all of the changes?

Answers on page 184.

Cozy Kids' Room

With busy kids living here, it's no wonder that this bright and welcoming room is changing. See if you can spot the ways.

Balancing Act

Can you spot all of the shifts between these two pictures?

Answers on page 185.

Song Swap

Sit right down, sing along, and start the search for differences.

Answers on page 185.

Crafted for Fun

We won't string you along—some of these changes may be tough to find!   **6 changes**

Pole Position

6 changes No playing around here—you'll have to get serious to find all of these changes.

Answers on page 185.

Hat Trick

Go ahead—throw your hat into the ring to see if you can solve this puzzle.   **6 changes**

Doll Developments

No need to skirt the issue—all you have to do is find the changes.

Answers on page 185.

Birthday Blowout

Find all of the changes, and you'll take the cake!

Off to the Ball Game

You'll have a ball solving this one,
so give it your best shot and find the changes!

Answers on page 186.

Getting Some Air

You'll need all feet on deck to solve this puzzle!

Makeup Tricks

One of these pictures received a bit of a makeover.
Examine her fantastical feline face, and find all the differences.

Answers on page 186.

King Tut Teaser

We're sure you can find the changes between these Egyptian kings.
We made them *pharaoh*-ly easy!

Answers on page 186.

Up a Tree

This puzzle poses a single knotty problem:
One of the pictures below is not like the others.

1

2

3

4

Answer on page 186.

A Couple of Clowns

We've made some modifications to this silly pair.
You're no Bozo—find them all!

Answers on page 187.

Make a Splash!

These water parks were the same, but then we let some things slide.
Dive right in to find the changes!

8 changes

Garage Band Goof

This jam session is jam-packed with changes.
But we're sure you'll find them all—you rock!

130

Answers on page 187.

Camel Creativity

These beautifully decorated camels are ready to be admired.
Just make sure you find the single change first!

1

2

3

4

Answer on page 187.

Happy Birthday to You

7 changes

Birthdays mean a new year and new changes,
so before you blow out the candles, scan these photos for what's different.

Supply the Answers

8 changes   Be sure to study these school supplies very closely. There will be a test!

Answers on page 187.

Easy as Pie

If you want to be of help in the kitchen,
take a close look at these pictures and note the variations.

7 changes

Knickknack Attack

8 changes

We wouldn't toy with you—we've made a lot of changes.
Can you find them all?

Answers on page 188.

Just Beachy

Don't just coast along—we're *shore* you can find all the differences if you try!   **7 changes**

How Sweet It Is

1 change

The celebration isn't over! Scan these favors to find
the one change that will make you the life of the party.

1

2

3

4

Answer on page 188.

Round 'em Up!

Giddyap to find all the changes in these pictures.

Barbecue Brainteaser

While the chef was flipping burgers, we flipped around
some things in these photos. Can you find the changes?

Play Your Cards Right

It's too early for slumber when there are games
to be played—and puzzles to be solved!

Answers on page 189.

Many, Many Masks

We've added a few changes to this picture.
Can you face the challenge?

Carnival Challenge

Ride a wave of good feelings as you spot all of the differences.

Answers on page 189.

Marble Mania!

Don't lose your marbles—just sort through them and find
the one hidden change in these pictures.

1

2

3

4

5

6

Toy Pole

The puppets on this pole are hanging in there.
Help untangle the strings to find all of the changes.

Answers on page 189.

Media Matters

You'll really feel plugged in once you've uncovered
all of the changes to this scene!

Come Along for the Ride

Can you spot the differences here?
You can hop on for a spin when you complete this puzzle!

Answers on page 190.

Classroom Changes

7 changes Take a look around this busy classroom as you attend to the changes
between pictures. Give yourself a gold star if you find them all!

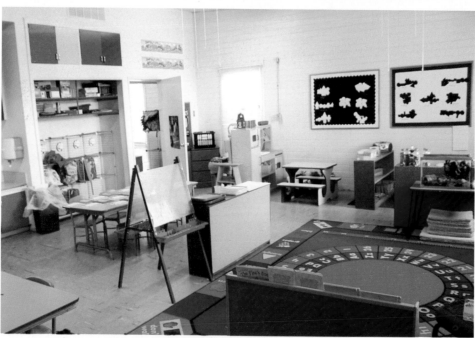

Answers on page 190.

Practice Makes Perfect

Hit all the right notes as you pick out all of the changes.

1 change

Tricky Treats

Taste the anticipation as you search these photos
for the single change among them.

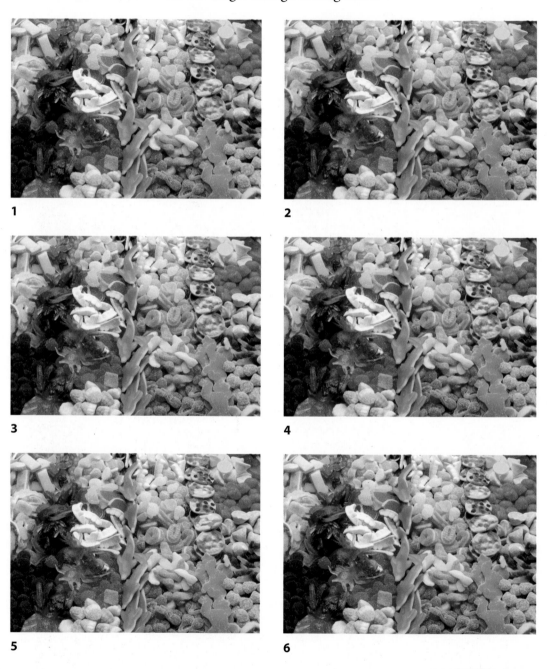

1

2

3

4

5

6

Answer on page 190.

A Mixed-Up Mess

We're sure you've heard Mom say this before—if you clean up your act, you should be able to locate all of the hidden changes!

8 changes

Fiery Finder

Get yourself out of hot water by finding all of the changes.

Answers on page 190.

Plentiful Panorama

We've woven plenty of changes through this scene. Can you find them all?   **7 changes**

Recorder Recital

This musical recital is a big event!
Be sure you're recording all of these changes.

Answers on page 191.

Fishy Frenzy

Go out on the prowl for changes in these underwater scenes.

7 changes

Miniskirt Mix-Up

These displays of stylish skirts are somewhat out of sync!
Use your keen fashion sense to spot the alterations.

Answers on page 191.

Thrilling Task

7 changes   We've added a whole carnival of changes to this scene. Can you find them all?

Answers on page 191.

Take a Number

Something about these photos doesn't add up—
maybe it's the single change we've hidden among them.

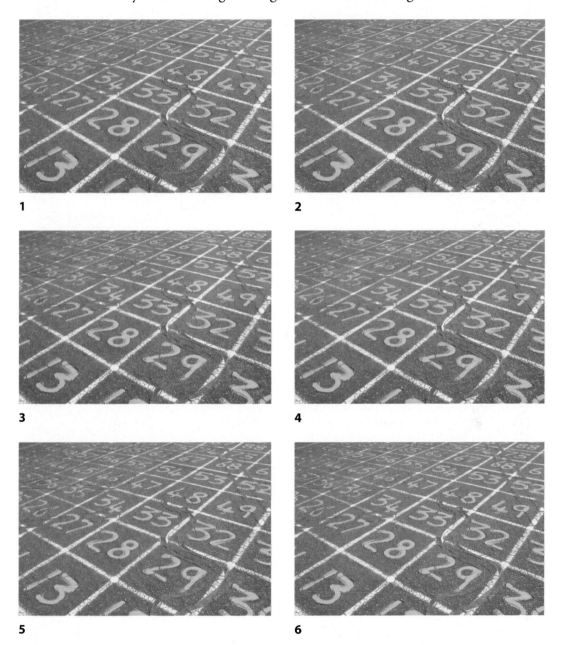

1

2

3

4

5

6

Toy Turnabout

Playtime has turned into an exercise of fun!
Spot the differences between these pictures.

Answers on page 192.

Down the Lazy River

Dive right in to find all the changes to this scene!

Answers on page 192.

8 changes

Hold Your Horses!

We've made some changes to one of these merry-go-rounds.
Do your best to find them before you get too dizzy.

Answers on page 192.

Blinded with Science

Put on your (scientific) thinking cap, and carefully develop a list of changes. **8 changes**

Answers on page 192.

Card Tricks

It's your turn! Show us your best trick by looking for
the differences between these pictures.

Answers on page 192.

A Lofty Goal

Climb the ladder of success as you locate all of these changes.

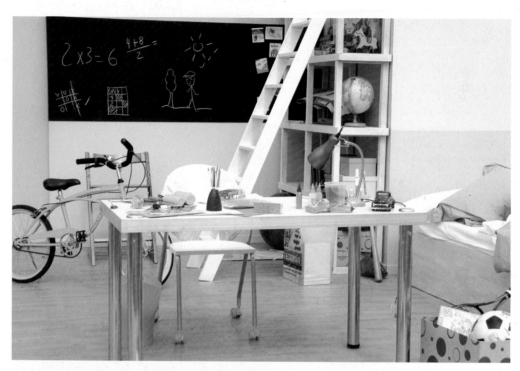

Answers on page 192.

LEVEL 1

Masterpiece Matching, *(page 5)* **1.** Flower picked; **2.** chimney smoke taller; **3.** window added; **4.** tree grew apples.

Toys on Parade, *(page 6)* **1.** Blue hat turned red; **2.** red piece covering spring; **3.** brown bead removed; **4.** giraffe stretched neck—he's trying to look over the other animals!

A New Sheriff in Town, *(page 7)* **1.** Pattern removed from gray blanket; **2.** star changed to circle; **3.** blue sleeping bag turned red; **4.** horse pole missing.

A Few of My Favorite Things, *(pages 8–9)* **1.** Blue block turned red; **2.** red-orange crayon missing; **3.** prince flipped upside down; **4.** blue crayon wrapper peeled back.

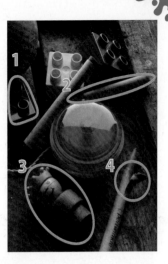

Queen of the Bubble Makers, *(page 10)* **1.** Tent pole missing; **2.** new bubble blown; **3.** green feather added; **4.** shirt sleeve longer—is she cold?

Bumblebee Mystery, *(page 11)* **1.** Cloud floated in; **2.** black rope missing—but how does it fly?; **3.** bee body lost its stripes; **4.** wing longer.

Piñata Party, *(page 12)* **1.** Pants longer; **2.** white hat grew larger; **3.** eye missing—someone took a good hit!; **4.** yellow sections turned green.

Monkeying Around, *(page 15)* **1.** Pigtail chopped off; **2.** pink shirt turned red; **3.** striped shirt longer; **4.** pole and hand missing—where did she go?

Greenhouse Guesser, *(page 13)* **1.** Silver can taller; **2.** flowerpot added; **3.** glove turned orange; **4.** girl's hair trimmed—she must have wanted a new look.

To the Sky and Back, *(pages 16–17)* **1.** Clouds floated away; **2.** circle now green; **3.** door missing—all that's left is the frame; **4.** another door missing—oh no, that's not safe!

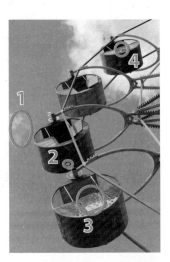

Seashore Stumper, *(page 14)* **1.** Umbrella edge in background disappeared in picture 2.

Art Astray, *(page 18)* **1.** Crayon rotated; **2.** cloudy day turned sunny; **3.** window missing; **4.** red shirt turned pink.

Tire Swing Teaser,
(pages 22–23)
1. Hand hiding behind tire; **2.** girl had a haircut; **3.** trees grew bushier; **4.** swimsuit lost white pattern.

Push/Pull Puzzle, *(page 19)* **1.** Striped shirt became solid; **2.** wagon wheel fell off—hope it doesn't tip over!; **3.** bar removed; **4.** white shoes and socks turned gray.

Playroom Puzzle, *(page 20)* **1.** Letter "F" became "E"; **2.** "K" flipped over; **3.** green circle added; **4.** tricycle gone—someone took it out for a spin!

Unburied Treasure, *(page 24)* **1.** We struck gold!—coin added in picture 3.

Costume Caper, *(page 21)* **1.** Watermelon seed added; **2.** flute longer; **3.** hat ties missing—hope it stays on!; **4.** drumstick end now square.

Summer Vacation Time!, *(page 25)* **1.** Pants turned black; **2.** Mom lost her bag; **3.** back window gone; **4.** flipper grew bigger—she'll swim in circles!

■ **Under My Umbrella,** *(page 26)* **1.** Flower removed; **2.** flower on raincoat grew; **3.** spoke missing; **4.** orange flower turned yellow.

■ **Gummi Game,** *(page 30)* **1.** Pink and white gummis switched in picture 1.

■ **Family Portrait,** *(page 27)* **1.** Two birds added to flock; **2.** marker missing; **3.** fence turned solid green; **4.** door and window added.

■ **Go Fly a Kite,** *(page 31)* **1.** Shirt and shorts switched colors; **2.** grass stalks clipped; **3.** red section of kite turned purple; **4.** person left—was the wind too much for her?

■ **River Walk,** *(pages 28–29)* **1.** Shirt buttons removed; **2.** overall straps missing; **3.** turtle's belly pattern gone; **4.** cuff rolled down.

■ **Shoe Swap,** *(page 32)* **1.** Shoe turned around; **2.** blue shoe's strap removed; **3.** polka dots missing; **4.** black polka dots turned white.

Tent Twist, *(page 33)* **1.** Flashlight missing— how will they find their way around in the dark?; **2.** triangle patch became circle; **3.** yellow sleeping bag now green; **4.** yellow panel turned light brown.

Guitar Guesser, *(pages 36–37)* **1.** Side of guitar turned white; **2.** frets (white lines) missing; **3.** white rectangle became green oval; **4.** lettering erased.

Dance Demonstration, *(page 34)* **1.** Hair bun grew in picture 5.

Chalk Caper, *(page 38)* **1.** Sleeve longer; **2.** door turned white; **3.** "9" became "8"; **4.** blue chalk outline added.

A Sandy Search, *(page 35)* **1.** Rocks grew; **2.** triangle-shaped eye became oval; **3.** more yellow spots added— is dino smiling now?; **4.** green scales turned yellow.

Freeze!, *(page 39)* **1.** Cap brim turned blue; **2.** blue section turned pink; **3.** butterfly added to shirt; **4.** silver piece on squirt gun removed.

■ **Still Life with Flowers,** *(page 40)* **1.** Green, yellow, and white stripes now red; **2.** wallflower added; **3.** round vase now square; **4.** cherry grew.

■ **Fishbowl Finder,** *(page 43)* **1.** Butterfly pin missing in picture 4.

■ **A Study in Blues,** *(page 41)* **1.** White band added to football; **2.** bedspread section now solid blue; **3.** bedpost taller; **4.** lamp shade turned yellow.

■ **The Family that Nests Together . . . ,** *(page 44)* **1.** Dad grew beard; **2.** boy's white collar turned black; **3.** Mom washed off blush makeup; **4.** sister moved next to Mom.

■ **Sock It to Me!,** *(page 42)* **1.** Sock missing—did it have to be washed?; **2.** stripe turned bright purple; **3.** toe turned orange; **4.** yellow stripes gone.

■ **Heart-ily Yours,** *(page 45)* **1.** Hand moved behind paper; **2.** flower sprouted; **3.** heart upside down; **4.** pencil longer.

LEVEL 2

■ **Children's Place,** *(page 46)* **1.** Green wall changed to yellow; **2.** porthole filled in; **3.** cutout added on ladder; **4.** basket moved; **5.** green shape changed to pink.

■ **Homework Helpers,** *(page 47)* **1.** Stack of books taller; **2.** book turned green; **3.** girl's ponytail grew—how long have they been studying?; **4.** pen missing from hand; **5.** colors flipped on notebook.

■ **Stamping Stampede,** *(pages 48–49)* **1.** Circle became star; **2.** more pink paint dripping over; **3.** circles turned white; **4.** stamp pattern added; **5.** blue paint can removed.

■ **Pillow Puzzler,** *(page 50)* **1.** Dots missing; **2.** zebra stripe gone; **3.** white bar changed to black; **4.** girl's knee moved; **5.** girl's hair trimmed.

■ **Dino Duel,** *(page 51)* **1.** Stegosaurus lost some spikes in picture 6.

■ **Kids' Carnival,** *(page 52)* **1.** Blue light turned pink; **2.** shape missing; **3.** letters erased; **4.** silver section taken off; **5.** extra claw makes ride that much more thrilling.

ANSWERS

Toy Task, *(pages 56–57)* **1.** Red handle turned blue; **2.** block taken away—someone wanted to play with it!; **3.** "B" became "X"; **4.** doll's eyes closed; **5.** dress turned orange.

Hitters' Huddle, *(page 53)* **1.** Pigtail grew; **2.** bat turned silver; **3.** belt changed to red; **4.** more lights added—so they can play at night?; **5.** number "5" turned upside down.

Skate Park, *(page 54)* **1.** End of railing gone; **2.** graffiti painted over; **3.** boy's shoe now all black; **4.** white outline changed to black; **5.** post added.

In a Class of Their Own, *(page 58)* **1.** Numbers "5" and "6" switched spots; **2.** logo on shirt removed; **3.** box turned green; **4.** yellow abacus beads turned red; **5.** blue chair gone.

Pasture Puzzler, *(page 55)* **1.** Cow left for more fertile ground in picture 2.

Meadow Mix-Up, *(page 59)* **1.** Daisy center now red; **2.** flower plucked; **3.** orange sleeve turned white; **4.** flowers multiplied; **5.** treetops grew.

■ Karaoke Kraze,

(pages 60–61)
1. Window enlarged—for a better view; **2.** guitar section (pickguard) turned red; **3.** stripes added to tights; **4.** "microphone" missing; **5.** belt doubled in size.

■ Beauty Mask Task, *(page 64)* **1.** Shutters filled in; **2.** braid snipped off; **3.** chair rail removed; **4.** pant pattern erased; **5.** mask turned green—uh-oh, did she leave it on too long?

■ Family Fun Find, *(page 62)* **1.** Hair grew—how long have they been coloring?; **2.** pencil moved left; **3.** cabinet added; **4.** mug turned green; **5.** someone was thirsty and drank some milk.

■ Up, Up, and Away!, *(page 65)* **1.** Window missing from lighthouse balloon; **2.** white row on balloon changed to blue; **3.** orange square turned blue; **4.** balloon floated away; **5.** another lighthouse balloon added on right.

■ Handy Candy Hunt,

(page 63)
1. Yellow candy added in picture 1.

■ Pencil Me In!, *(page 66)* **1.** Blue marker added; **2.** light purple pencil sharpener added; **3.** knife blade lengthened and black rectangle moved down—best to be careful!; **4.** cap removed; **5.** leaf blew away.

■ **Coin Count,** *(page 67)* **1.** Gray section added; **2.** blanket removed; **3.** coin spent; **4.** soccer piggy bank's plug moved down; **5.** more coins added.

■ **Bunny Brainteaser,** *(page 68)* **1.** Ball enlarged in picture 5.

■ **Girls' Night In,** *(page 69)* **1.** Spoon removed—how will she scoop up her favorite flavor?; **2.** chocolate and sprinkles added; **3.** green bowl turned yellow; **4.** cabinet door boarded over; **5.** white undershirt raised.

■ **Painting Party,** *(page 70)* **1.** Brush dipping into blue paint instead of red; **2.** brush taken away—hopefully for cleaning!; **3.** cup moved down; **4.** petal added to flower; **5.** hand appeared—looks like everyone wants to paint.

■ **Multiply and Divide,** *(page 71)* **1.** Stickers added to folder; **2.** card flipped around; **3.** snack eaten—homework makes everyone hungry!; **4.** "9" became "27"; **5.** crayon added.

■ **Traveling Team,** *(pages 72–73)* **1.** Ear curved up; **2.** soccer ball now solid white; **3.** seat line erased; **4.** belt turned black; **5.** marker removed.

■ Doggie's New Tricks, *(page 74)* **1.** Tree removed; **2.** shadows gone; **3.** doggie's toy missing; **4.** dog moved; **5.** Dad's sweater turned dark gray.

■ Coney Island Cones, *(page 77)* **1.** Sign turned sideways in picture 3.

■ A Sweeping Performance, *(page 75)* **1.** Cabinet knobs lowered; **2.** skirt longer; **3.** glass added; **4.** stitching removed; **5.** chair leg longer.

■ When It Rains, It Pours, *(pages 78–79)* **1.** Umbrella bigger—better for staying dry!; **2.** hood turned blue; **3.** pocket flap turned green; **4.** umbrella character missing; **5.** flower added to shirt.

■ Studio Search, *(page 76)* **1.** Rainbow upside down; **2.** chalkboard moved right; **3.** top of chair removed; **4.** addition problem made vertical; **5.** paint tin added.

■ Geographical Goof, *(page 80)* **1.** Books added to stack; **2.** map turned upside down; **3.** buttons turned black; **4.** U-neck became V-neck; **5.** skirt turned dark brown.

Guinea Pig Guesser, *(page 81)* **1.** Dark bricks removed; **2.** guinea pig facing right; **3.** other guinea pig snuck back inside; **4.** brown patch added; **5.** window appeared—for a better view?

A Quick Study, *(page 84)* **1.** Paper removed; **2.** pencil container turned blue; **3.** border turned green; **4.** pencil vanished; **5.** poster disappeared.

Stuffed Shelves, *(page 82)* **1.** Pattern missing; **2.** stuffed animal taller; **3.** red bear turned brown; **4.** "I Love You" on feet erased; **5.** shelf extended—to fit more toys.

Guitar Heroines, *(page 85)* **1.** Clouds removed; **2.** bracelet switched wrists; **3.** pillow square turned green; **4.** braid trimmed—did it get in the way of her playing?; **5.** lamp base widened.

Splash-tacular!, *(page 83)* **1.** Raft longer; **2.** foot went underwater—so much splashing!; **3.** horn removed; **4.** white wavy stripe added; **5.** white paw print added.

Turtle Teaser, *(page 86)* **1.** Orange triangle became circle in picture 1.

LEVEL 3

■ Block Party, *(page 87)* **1.** Top white piece turned blue; **2.** sleeve changed to solid blue; **3.** yellow piece removed; **4.** bottom yellow block erased; **5.** yellow block turned red—what's with those yellow blocks?; **6.** blue block also turned red.

■ Kitchen Renovations, *(page 88)* **1.** Dish disappeared; **2.** can added; **3.** knob changed; **4.** sticker moved right; **5.** blue pot turned red; **6.** cabinet handle grew longer.

■ Skate-o-Rama, *(page 89)* **1.** Watch removed; **2.** window filled in; **3.** person went home; **4.** wheel end now white; **5.** rail section missing; **6.** umbrella bigger—for more shade on a sunny day!

■ Costume Party, *(pages 90–91)* **1.** Knife taken away—for safety, of course!; **2.** yellow blower became green; **3.** yellow and white icing changed to pink with a red candy; **4.** "Happy Birthday" flipped around; **5.** yellow flower turned purple; **6.** fringe on sleeve gone.

■ Dolly Doozy, *(page 92)* **1.** Yellow strings turned red; **2.** bee's nose turned black; **3.** black stripe gone; **4.** doll's bangs trimmed; **5.** another row of wooden balls appeared; **6.** design missing from doll's dress.

■ Splatter Pattern, *(page 93)* **1.** Paint jar flipped around and moved to bottom of splash in picture 4.

ANSWERS

Sledding Switcheroo, *(page 94)* **1.** Ski pole moved right; **2.** scarf blown away—hope he doesn't get too cold!; **3.** rope turned all black; **4.** sled rail uncovered; **5.** loop widened; **6.** rail extended.

Boot Shoot, *(page 95)* **1.** Soles turned solid red; **2.** dress longer; **3.** red line added; **4.** hearts flipped upside down; **5.** circle now a star; **6.** toes turned black.

Hula Hunt, *(page 96)* **1.** Roof beam removed; **2.** white trim added; **3.** flower fence (trellis) turned into solid white wall; **4.** hula hoop turned blue; **5.** tree behind house chopped down; **6.** dark shadow extended.

Study Hall, *(page 97)* **1.** Purple-outlined note added; **2.** girl's hair snipped off; **3.** signs switched spots; **4.** chairs joined to make a bench; **5.** yellow signs lined up; **6.** boy's buttonhole missing.

Soccer Shuffle, *(pages 98–99)* **1.** Shorts became pants; **2.** blue stripe turned red; **3.** trophy base now circular; **4.** trophy top curved to right; **5.** hole formed in net—it was quite a kick!; **6.** medal ribbon shortened.

Googly-Eyed Game, *(page 100)* **1.** Hole filled in; **2.** googly eye added; **3.** letter button appeared; **4.** cross turned upside down; **5.** star removed; **6.** eyebrows added.

Canoe Caper, *(page 101)* **1.** Rock added; **2.** silver strip added to front of canoe; **3.** tree chopped down; **4.** another tree grew; **5.** paddle attached on left—so they can go faster!; **6.** white trim extended.

Guitar Greats, *(pages 104–105)* **1.** Guitar end (headstock) disappeared; **2.** dark brown trim (pickguard) moved to other side of hole; **3.** white labels missing; **4.** worn patch moved up; **5.** guitars switched spots; **6.** chair base missing—how is he balancing?

Fountain Fluke, *(page 102)* **1.** Aqua trim painted gray; **2.** design on shirt removed; **3.** spout base squared off; **4.** ice cream bar gone—did it melt already?; **5.** post grew taller; **6.** shorts became jeans.

Candy, Candy in a Dish . . . , *(page 106)* **1.** Number "2" flipped right side up; **2.** orange candy turned blue; **3.** yellow candy added; **4.** green candy turned red; **5.** brown stripe removed; **6.** black candy added.

Robot Parade, *(page 103)* **1.** Antenna added in picture 1.

A Puzzling Event, *(page 107)* **1.** Flowers and vase taller; **2.** stripe turned dark brown; **3.** puzzle piece added; **4.** "21" became "12"; **5.** vertical dividers missing; **6.** chair seat extended.

■ Lane Change, *(page 108)* **1.** Ceiling vent added; **2.** black section longer; **3.** lettering erased; **4.** red section turned black; **5.** stripe painted over; **6.** ball added in middle lane—but who threw it?

■ Plush Toy Puzzle, *(page 111)* **1.** Ribbon missing; **2.** left eye patch added; **3.** carrots eaten— some bunny must have been hungry; **4.** white part of centipede's foot changed to black; **5.** dog now looking sideways; **6.** doll frowning.

■ School Bus Search, *(page 109)* **1.** Red section on backpack turned black; **2.** girl took strap off shoulder; **3.** glasses taken off—hope she can see clearly!; **4.** rear doorframe gone; **5.** necklace bead added; **6.** window bar appeared.

■ Landscaper's Challenge, *(page 112)* **1.** Lamp lowered; **2.** flowerpot added; **3.** reflection missing; **4.** flower picked; **5.** pink flowers turned red; **6.** branch trimmed.

■ Take It Easy, *(page 110)* **1.** Knickknacks missing; **2.** frame taken off wall; **3.** number "5" became "8"; **4.** belt turned white; **5.** candy wrapper removed; **6.** pillow missing.

■ Cozy Kids' Room, *(page 113)* **1.** Blue circle turned green; **2.** green tieback now pink; **3.** shelf replaced with drawer—good place for a diary?; **4.** chair wheel missing; **5.** magazine moved left; **6.** white design added to wall.

■ **Balancing Act,** *(pages 114–115)* **1.** Tree sprouted; **2.** writing on jacket gone; **3.** white stripe missing; **4.** grass grew; **5.** light from post missing; **6.** strap longer.

■ **Pole Position,** *(page 118)* **1.** Post toppers switched; **2.** arched bar removed; **3.** lion facing right; **4.** yellow roller became square; **5.** green palm tree topper turned yellow; **6.** more yellow flowers bloomed.

■ **Song Swap,** *(page 116)* **1.** Tent flipped—you have to get in on the left side now; **2.** boy's hair grew over ear; **3.** blue T-shirt turned white; **4.** boy went home; **5.** blue shoe turned pink; **6.** cup removed.

■ **Hat Trick,** *(page 119)* **1.** Letters on cap erased; **2.** shirt longer; **3.** sunglasses removed; **4.** hat decoration moved to left; **5.** orange flower added; **6.** hat top now square.

■ **Crafted for Fun,** *(page 117)* **1.** Cheek turned all red—doll must be extra embarrassed about something!; **2.** shoe missing; **3.** tongue back in mouth; **4.** white hair turned green; **5.** shoe flipped around; **6.** doll's collar painted blue.

■ **Doll Developments,** *(page 120)* **1.** Braid moved in front of shoulder; **2.** purple flower bloomed; **3.** blue stripe removed; **4.** leaf grew; **5.** flowers all white; **6.** red skirt turned blue.

■ **Makeup Tricks,** *(pages 124–125)* **1.** Beads added; **2.** whisker wiped away; **3.** white streak added; **4.** another dot painted on; **5.** more whiskers grew; **6.** beads fell off.

■ **Birthday Blowout,** *(page 121)* **1.** Green fringe added; **2.** gift tag removed; **3.** green ribbon grew; **4.** "6" became "8"; **5.** frosting rose added—for more sweetness; **6.** yellow and blue party blowers switched.

■ **Off to the Ball Game,** *(page 122)* **1.** More fake grass laid to cover asphalt; **2.** roof raised; **3.** green window added; **4.** pointy roof became square; **5.** chimney moved left; **6.** ball added.

■ **King Tut Teaser,** *(page 126)* **1.** Red light gone; **2.** brown stripe missing; **3.** support bars vanished—hope Tut is stable!; **4.** gold area turned green; **5.** turquoise stripe disappeared; **6.** red lights now blue.

■ **Getting Some Air,** *(page 123)* **1.** Red roof removed; **2.** black stripe turned white; **3.** pole added for extra support; **4.** tree chopped down; **5.** building taller; **6.** windows added.

■ **Up a Tree,** *(page 127)* **1.** Red flower on shirt turned blue in picture 2.

LEVEL 4

■ **Camel Creativity,** *(page 131)* **1.** Yellow flower added in picture 1.

■ **A Couple of Clowns,** *(page 128)* **1.** Clown's tag moved up; **2.** orange square turned purple; **3.** pin missing; **4.** red makeup on bottom lip removed; **5.** red nose turned blue; **6.** white button now purple; **7.** earring taken off.

■ **Make a Splash!,** *(page 129)* **1.** Railing turned green; **2.** dome taken down; **3.** poles added—to hold up the slide, of course!; **4.** post missing; **5.** lounge chairs switched spots; **6.** green pole now blue; **7.** red spots removed from mushroom top; **8.** roof turned yellow.

■ **Happy Birthday to You,** *(pages 132–133)* **1.** Red daisy changed to yellow; **2.** confetti moved down; **3.** blower gone; **4.** somebody ate the purple flower; **5.** smiley face removed; **6.** black band changed to white; **7.** yellow confetti moved down and right.

■ **Garage Band Goof,** *(page 130)* **1.** Yellow tape longer; **2.** strips on drum gone; **3.** tie now red; **4.** guitar lost volume knobs—maybe Mom doesn't want them to get too loud; **5.** circle on shirt turned blue; **6.** tattoo removed; **7.** garden tool gone; **8.** case lost snaps.

■ **Supply the Answers,** *(page 134)* **1.** Marker vanished—must be a *magic* marker!; **2.** holes added; **3.** roll of tape smaller; **4.** ruler shortened; **5.** eraser moved right; **6.** notebook turned orange; **7.** red and blue crayons switched places; **8.** end of pencil became solid black.

Easy as Pie, *(page 135)* **1.** Label turned black; **2.** some little turkey removed the stuffing!; **3.** branch snipped off; **4.** apple slice moved left; **5.** zucchini eaten; **6.** nuts added to bowl—what a nutty idea; **7.** neckline of shirt turned light blue.

Knickknack Attack, *(page 136)* **1.** Nose turned red; **2.** nose rotated; **3.** shell added; **4.** heart moved left; **5.** puzzle piece missing; **6.** glasses removed; **7.** shape rotated; **8.** eyes closed.

Just Beachy, *(page 137)* **1.** Towel flipped; **2.** kid paddled away; **3.** shorts became capri pants; **4.** straps missing; **5.** blue designs gone; **6.** sandals moved to right; **7.** rock washed ashore.

■ How Sweet It Is, *(page 138)* **1.** Heart erased from lollipop in picture 4.

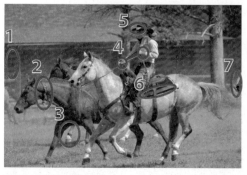

■ Round 'em Up!, *(page 139)* **1.** Two more rails added; **2.** horse's collar taken off; **3.** horse's leg moved up; **4.** red cuffs on shirt turned white; **5.** hatband now red; **6.** brown strap turned black; **7.** horse out of the picture—he lost by a nose!

■ Barbecue Brainteaser, *(pages 140–141)* **1.** Hair bow disappeared; **2.** yellow shirt turned green; **3.** pocket stripes changed direction; **4.** stack of cups taller; **5.** napkins turned blue; **6.** tree trimmed; **7.** blue bandana now red; **8.** person went home.

■ **Play Your Cards Right,** *(page 142)*
1. Curtain widened; **2.** pillow moved left; **3.** butterfly flew off pajamas; **4.** bow appeared; **5.** cards disappeared—hope they're not up her sleeve!; **6.** butterfly added to wallpaper; **7.** sleeve lengthened.

■ **Marble Mania!,** *(page 145)* **1.** Swirl gone in picture 6.

■ **Many, Many Masks,** *(page 143)* **1.** Mask lost some teeth; **2.** eye outline turned red; **3.** eye outline now green; **4.** fringe deleted; **5.** zigzag added; **6.** nose turned white; **7.** hatband now solid green.

■ **Toy Pole,** *(page 146)* **1.** Hand replaced with circular paw; **2.** black stripe deleted; **3.** cow *moo*-ved on; **4.** strings missing—how are puppets hanging on?; **5.** yellow shoe turned orange; **6.** pink tentacle deleted; **7.** shark tail gone.

■ **Carnival Challenge,** *(page 144)* **1.** Tree grew; **2.** red reflectors added—for safety; **3.** white design erased; **4.** light added; **5.** car disappeared; **6.** arrow pointing right; **7.** stripes straightened out.

■ **Media Matters,** *(page 147)* **1.** Reflection missing; **2.** foam bar extended; **3.** cord added; **4.** cup bigger; **5.** circular speaker now square; **6.** carpet track design removed; **7.** faucet missing; **8.** picture removed.

■ **Come Along for the Ride,** *(pages 148–149)*
1. Cloud appeared; **2.** bucket's circle gone; **3.** blue top turned purple; **4.** purple car now yellow; **5.** gold circle turned green; **6.** bird design changed direction; **7.** red flag missing.

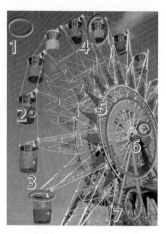

■ **Tricky Treats,** *(page 152)* **1.** Green decorations picked off candy piece in picture 5.

■ **Classroom Changes,** *(page 150)* **1.** Chair taken away; **2.** poster added to wall; **3.** design gone from rug; **4.** drawer pulls missing; **5.** another book added; **6.** red strip lengthened; **7.** design appeared on board.

■ **A Mixed-Up Mess,** *(page 153)* **1.** T-shirt taken down a rung; **2.** monkey added; **3.** ribbons switched spots; **4.** hangers missing; **5.** purse straps gone; **6.** blue object added; **7.** poster disappeared; **8.** water bottle recycled.

■ **Practice Makes Perfect,** *(page 151)* **1.** Tag moved to left; **2.** gold bar removed; **3.** polka dots erased; **4.** black bar turned vertical; **5.** guitar point shorter and rounded; **6.** case added to stack; **7.** red panel added.

■ **Fiery Finder,** *(page 154)* **1.** Grass grew over sidewalk; **2.** white sections turned red; **3.** "3" flip-flopped; **4.** bracelet taken off; **5.** front wheel gone—hope he doesn't tip over!; **6.** smoke became fluffy cloud; **7.** taillight removed.

■ **Miniskirt Mix-Up,** *(pages 158–159)* **1.** Pink belt threads longer; **2.** belt turned yellow; **3.** flowers disappeared; **4.** pink ruffles now red; **5.** white flowers added; **6.** butterfly buckle gone; **7.** fruit designs switched places; **8.** bow taken away.

■ **Plentiful Panorama,** *(page 155)* **1.** Vine grew and added leaves; **2.** skirt lengthened; **3.** flower upside down; **4.** red shoes turned blue; **5.** seed design removed; **6.** curlicue snipped off; **7.** flower added.

■ **Recorder Recital,** *(page 156)* **1.** Apple added; **2.** outlet removed; **3.** support bar shortened; **4.** music upside down—how will they play?; **5.** socks pulled up; **6.** eraser added; **7.** pillow colors switched.

■ **Thrilling Task,** *(page 160)* **1.** Bar removed; **2.** white umbrella section now red; **3.** "C" became "T"; **4.** white structure gone; **5.** tent top flattened; **6.** Ferris wheel center enlarged; **7.** ropes and chairs missing.

■ **Fishy Frenzy,** *(page 157)* **1.** Coral removed; **2.** fin missing; **3.** two fish swam away—smart move!; **4.** blue fish added; **5.** orange fish appeared; **6.** seaweed floated away; **7.** fish turned around.

■ **Take a Number,** *(page 161)* **1.** "45" became "54" in picture 2.

Toy Turnabout, *(page 162)* **1.** Window turned into a wall; **2.** green piece taken away; **3.** yellow sleeve end changed to purple; **4.** red car moved down; **5.** blocks added; **6.** white line appeared; **7.** yellow pole now red.

Blinded with Science, *(page 165)* **1.** Yellow piece turned green; **2.** white instrument discarded; **3.** green liquid level raised; **4.** more stripes added to tie; **5.** disk moved left; **6.** star deleted; **7.** red liquid level raised; **8.** neck of beaker shortened.

Down the Lazy River, *(page 163)* **1.** Grass grew over dirt; **2.** rock expanded; **3.** pole removed; **4.** inner tube added—more kids can join!; **5.** rock taller; **6.** flowers turned white; **7.** blue sign added.

Card Tricks, *(pages 166–167)* **1.** Boy moved his foot; **2.** objects switched places; **3.** undershirt turned black; **4.** his cards disappeared—what a trick!; **5.** deck moved down; **6.** basket moved left; **7.** candleholder deleted; **8.** glass piece moved up a shelf.

Hold Your Horses!, *(page 164)* **1.** Horse's sash turned green; **2.** gold design added to base; **3.** flag turned yellow; **4.** green spot vanished; **5.** flower added; **6.** green spot turned blue; **7.** part of carousel changed to pink; **8.** pole appeared.

A Lofty Goal, *(page 168)* **1.** "2 x 3 = 6" became "2 x 4 = 8"; **2.** seat backward; **3.** garbage can widened; **4.** card moved; **5.** be careful!—wheel removed; **6.** lamp rotated right; **7.** tennis racket gone—someone's off to play!